ThE FRicTiON AnD MOTION COMMOTION

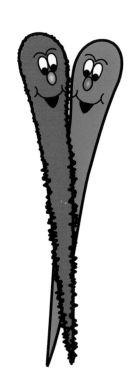

KlevaKids.com Inc

KlevaKids.com Inc

Presents

THE FRICTION AND MOTION COMMOTION

This colorful story introduces the concept of friction being present wherever there is motion. The character Motion represents any type of movement. The character Friction represents any resistance to movement. Together they embody the concept that whenever there is movement, there is resistance to movement.

The above statements are purely informational. The purpose of the book is not to teach, but to expose concepts. Read the book to a child and just allow the story to be enjoyed.

For more titles,visit our website at www.klevakids.com

How could nature have arranged

two eggs that looked so very strange?

Bumps on the side and lumps on top,

these egg things were about to pop.

One egg gave a wiggle,

followed by a wobble.

It first creaked,

then finally cracked.

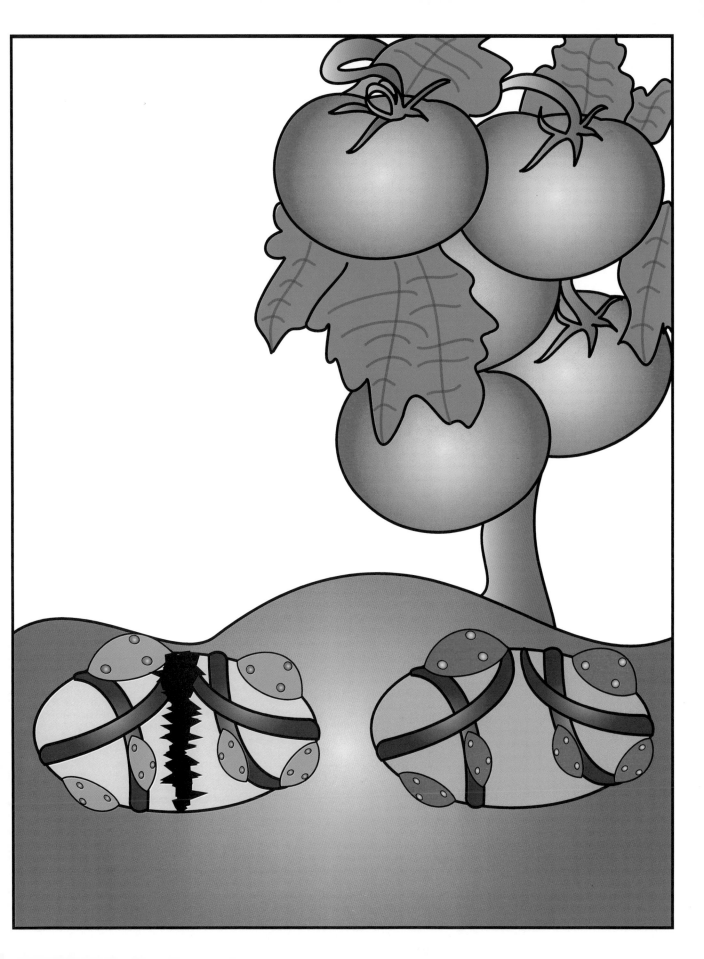

A puff of smoke came out of the crack.

Did something come out and go right back?

This thing came out like a blur.

Surely it would cause an enormous stir.

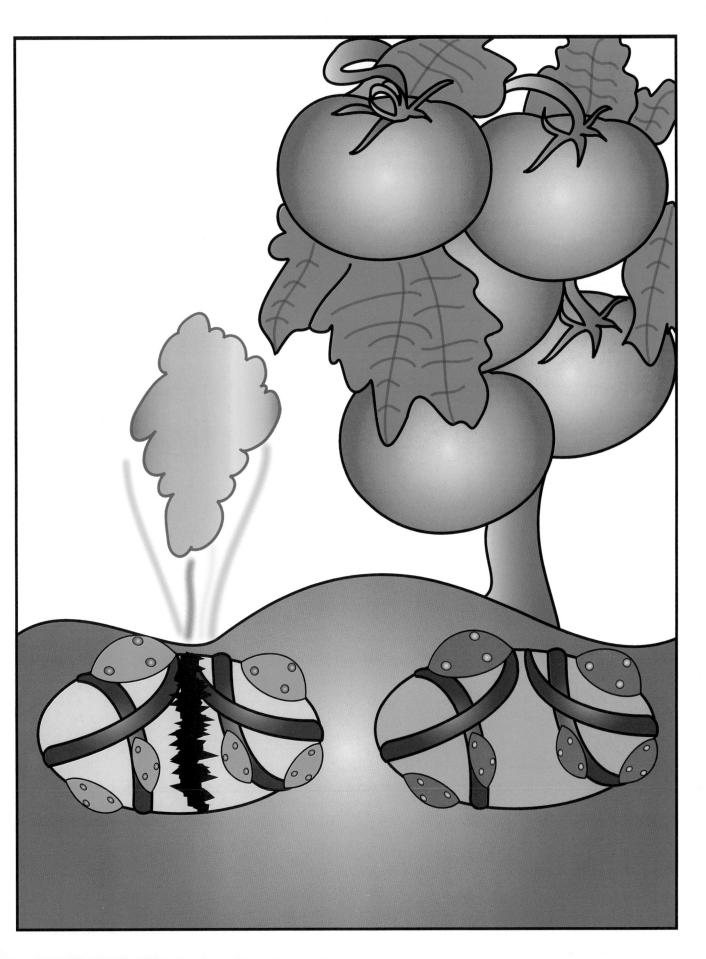

Whatever it was, it moved so fast.

It burst through tomatoes with a blast.

It moved so recklessly in a flash.

No doubt it had to crash.

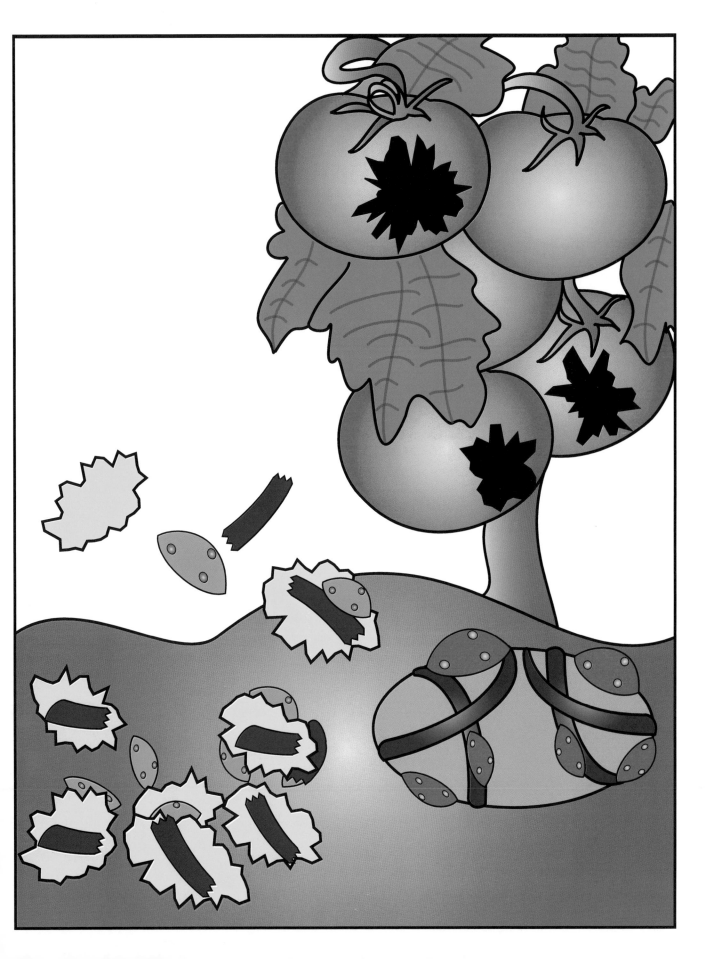

Here was Motion

causing all the commotion.

Some things are fast, but Motion was faster.

Yet, stopping meant pure disaster.

A titter, then a tatter,

what else was the matter?

The other egg cracked, two eyes stared.

Something was in there, was it scared?

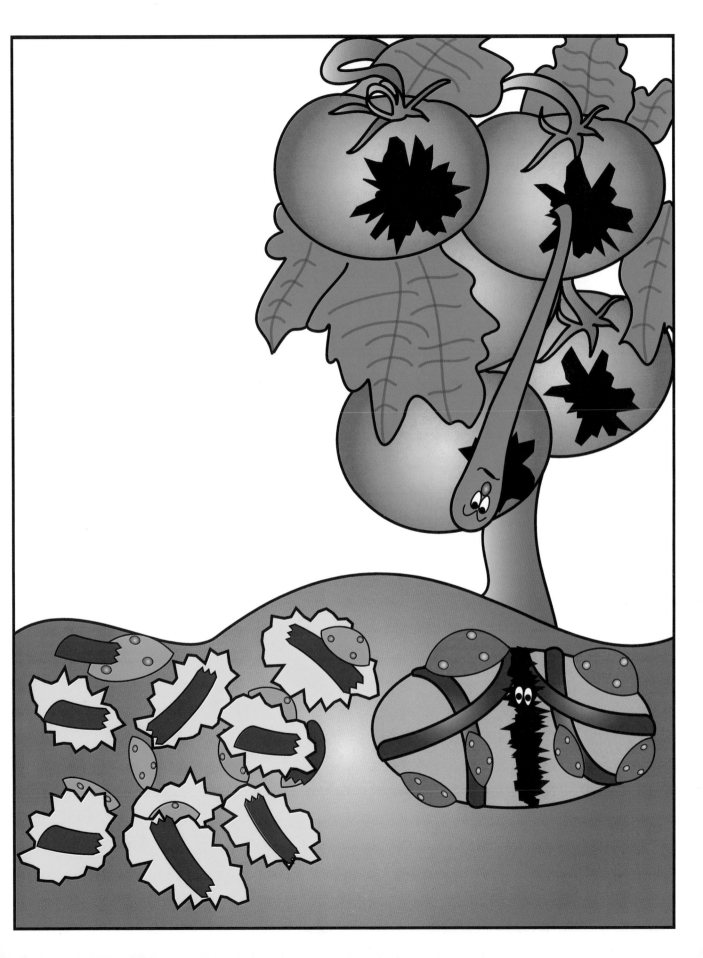

This was Friction amid the debris.

Friction was sad, sad as can be.

Here was Friction surrounded by rubble,

unable to move, that was the trouble.

Motion then slid past a leaf

and onto Friction in disbelief.

Motion landed on Friction with a jolt.

To get off, Motion tried to bolt.

They took off together filled with fright

and as they flew, it was such a delight.

Passing green beans, they did not talk

and flew, while friction could not walk.

Alas, it was time to take the test.

Exactly how would they come to rest.

Gliding gently toward a pumpkin top

this is where they would try to stop.

Once again a look of surprise and shock,

They took off and landed without a knock.

Motion made them go, but could not stop.

Friction made them land without a plop.

While resting, they thought it through.

Try again is what they had to do.

It was so marvelous to see them try.

Off they went to gleefully fly.

Now it was time for them to stop.

Friction on bottom and Motion on top.

Back to the pumpkin both did glide.

Their landing ended a joyful ride.

Now all can see,

their hearts filled with glee,

together they will be,

Friction and Motion happily.

THE END

Made in the USA
Lexington, KY
14 February 2012